E
BA

Balian, Lorna

Amelia's nine lives

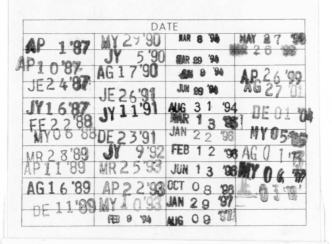

DATE			
AP 1 '87	MY 29 '90	MAR 8 '94	MAY 27 '98
AP 10 '87	JY 5 '90	MAR 29 '94	MAY 26 '98
JE 24 '87	AG 17 '90	AM 9 '94	AP 26 '99
JY 16 '87	JE 26 '91	JUN 28 '94	AG 27 01
FE 22 '88	JY 11 '91	AUG 31 '94	DE 01 '04
MY 06 '88	DE 23 '91	MAR 13 '95	
MR 28 '89	JY 9 '92	JAN 22 '96	MY 05 05
AP 11 '89	MR 25 '93	FEB 12 '96	AG 01 13
AG 16 '89	AP 22 '93	JUN 13 '96	MY 06 17
DE 11 '89	MY 10 '93	OCT 08 '96	03 19
	FEB 9 '94	JAN 29 '97	
		AUG 09 '97	

© THE BAKER & TAYLOR CO.

AMELIA'S NINE LIVES

AMELIA'S NINE LIVES

LORNA BALIAN

ABINGDON PRESS

NASHVILLE

Library of Congress Cataloging in Publication Data

Balian, Lorna.
  Amelia's nine lives.
  Summary: Nine of Nora's friends and relatives bring her replacement cats after she loses her
beloved Amelia, but there is still one surprise in store.
  [1. Cats—Fiction]   I. Title.
PZ7.B1978A1   1986   [E]   85-30835

ISBN 0-687-01250-3 (alk. paper)

This book is printed on acid-free paper.

Creative and technical adviser—John Balian

Manufactured in the United States of America

For Tansy with love

This is Nora and her cat, Amelia.
Nora loved Amelia.
She loved the way Amelia looked,
and purred, and smelled, and felt.

On Friday Amelia disappeared.
Nora looked everywhere.
Nora's mama looked everywhere.

Nora's papa looked everywhere.
Nora's brother, Ernie, looked everywhere.
No Amelia!

Nora started to bawl.
"Don't cry, dear," said Mama.
"Amelia will come back.
Cats have nine lives, you know."
Nora bawled louder.
Papa said, "For heaven's sake!
Stop crying! Your mama's right.
The cat will come back!"
"How can cats have nine lives?" asked Ernie.
Nobody answered him.
Nora was howling too loud to hear if they had.
Everyone looked for Amelia again—
in places they hadn't thought of before.
No Amelia!

This went on for days:
crying and looking—
bawling and looking—
howling and looking.
No Amelia!

On Tuesday Ernie asked the neighbors
if they'd seen Amelia.
Mama placed a notice in the newspaper.
Papa put a sign on the lawn.
Nora cried.
"Don't cry, dear," said Mama.
"Amelia will come back.
Cats have nine lives, you know."

On Wednesday Grandma came.
"I found Amelia," she said.
"Thank heavens!" said Papa.
"Thank heavens!" said Ernie.
"Thank Grandma," said Mama.
"Thank you, Grandma," said Nora,
but she didn't stop crying.

On Thursday Mrs. Perkins came.
So did Uncle George.
They both had Amelias.
"Thank Mrs. Perkins
and Uncle George, dear," said Mama.
"Thank you, Mrs. Perkins.
Thank you, Uncle George," said Nora,
but she didn't stop crying.

On Friday the mailman came.
So did Aunt Lucy,
and Mr. Olson,
and cousin Jake.
They all had Amelias.
"Thank everyone, dear," said Mama.
"Thank you, everyone," said Nora,
but she didn't stop crying.

On Saturday the paperboy came.
So did Grandpa.
They both brought Amelias.
"Thank them, dear," said Mama.
"Thank you," said Nora,
but she didn't stop crying.

"You were right, Mama.
Cats do have nine lives," said Ernie.
"I'm going to the store for more cat food," said Mama.
"Good heavens!" said Papa.

On Sunday Nora stopped crying.
"Mama! Papa! Ernie!
Amelia came back!
I know she's Amelia!
She looks like Amelia!
She purrs like Amelia!
She smells like Amelia!
She feels like Amelia . . .

and she's got four kittens!"
said Nora with a big smile.
"Good heavens!" said Papa.
"Good heavens!" said Mama.
"Does that mean cats have fourteen lives?" asked Ernie.
Nobody answered him.

On Monday Ernie asked the neighbors
if they'd like a cat.
Mama placed a notice in the newspaper.
Papa put a sign on the lawn.